For Ceira — Best wishes & lots of love, Aileen Paterson

Maisie's Mystery Tour

Morningside basked in the palmy days of Summer. Kittens frolicked in the Park, played cricket or tennis, or bobbed their tiny yachts on the bright sparkling waters of the Pond; adult cats donned shorts and tee-shirts and snoozed the afternoons away on deck-chairs and airbeds, or relaxed in a leisurely game of bowls; even Maisie Mackenzie's Granny acknowledged the change of season, by opening the window of her front room and allowing the distant hum of traffic to float in on the warm breeze. Only Maisie was gloomy.

She slumped in Granny's big chair, fiddling distractedly with a tangle of wool; or sat for hours over a jigsaw puzzle, pieces scattered over the kitchen table, making little effort to put the picture together. She mumped and moaned, scowled and groaned, whenever Granny asked her to pop down to the shops, or set the table. All day long, she fretted and fidgeted. At night, she tossed and turned in her bed. She was absolutely, utterly, BORED.

"What's up, pet," asked Granny one morning, beginning to worry that perhaps Maisie was sickening for something. She had never seen the little kitten so listless before.

"Och, Granny," replied Maisie, "I'm fed up. All my friends are away for their holidays and there's nothing to do."

"Holidays aren't all they're cracked up to be, Maisie," said Granny, trying to cheer her up. "Strange food, strange beds, strange sights. I really don't know why folks can't be content with their own firesides."

Just then, the letterbox clattered and they heard the postie whistle as he made his way back down the stairs. Maisie trudged through to the lobby and collected the mail. At the kitchen table, she spread it out. There were three postcards and a letter, all for her. The postcards were from her three friends, and she read them to Granny.

Flora's was a picture of Paris by night.

"France is fun — I have been up the Eiffel Tower and had frogs' legs and snails for dinner."

"Dearie me," gasped Granny. "That's terrible! The poor soul will *not* be well."

Archie's postcard was from Blackpool.

"Lots to do here — sand, sea and funfairs. Great view from the top of Blackpool Tower."

"They say it's an awful crowded place," sniffed Granny. "Nothing but bright lights and noise. Poor Archie."

Love to
Maisie
from
Daddy
xxx

Effie was in London.

"Went to the Waxworks, and the Zoo, and the Theatre, and the Tower of London — having a great time."

"She'll be quite worn out by the time she gets home, the wee mite," said Granny, shaking her head and tut-tutting.

Maisie stared at the three postcards. She felt very glum.

"Have you forgotten your letter, Maisie?" asked Granny.

It was from her Daddy. Maisie opened and read it.

"Dear Maisie, I have had a short break from my explorations. I went on a paddle-boat on a great lake, where there were lots of hippopotamuses and crocodiles. A fierce storm blew up and we thought the boat would sink, but it managed to reach safety. Then I visited an ancient site, said by locals to be haunted. I didn't see any ghosts. It was a nice little holiday. Lots of Love, Daddy."

There was a photograph of her Daddy, wearing tropical gear, looking very relaxed and rested.

"My word," said Granny, shaking her head again. "Storms and wild animals and ghosts. That isn't my idea of a holiday. I'm glad we live in a civilised country — you wouldn't find me going anywhere like that, not for all the tea in China!"

Maisie put her letter away, and stood the postcards and the photo on the mantlepiece. She felt quite miserable.

"I wish *I* could have a holiday," she said grumpily, adding, "I think I'll just go back to bed." And so she did.

Later that day, Granny took Maisie on her knee, in the big chair. Sun streamed in the window. The flowers in the window box nodded in the breeze. A lone bee buzzed about them.

"Cheer up, Maisie," said Granny. "Mrs McKitty and I had a 'thinking cup' of tea and put our heads together. We are going to have a wee holiday. I've booked seats on a Mystery Tour for tomorrow, and you're sure to have an adventure then."

"What's a Mystery Tour," asked Maisie, puzzled.

"You go for a run in a big bus, all day, and nobody knows where it is going — except the driver, and he won't tell. It's always a nice surprise when you arrive." Maisie brightened up at this. It sounded like fun. She quizzed Granny about Mystery Tours and discovered that they had been all the rage when Granny was a little kitten. Granny told Maisie about open-topped charabancs, and Tours that had ended up in the most unexpected places.

"The nice thing about a Mystery Tour," said Granny, smiling, "is that it always brings you home again."

The following morning, Maisie and Granny bustled about the flat, preparing for the day out. Into Granny's big shopping bag went lots of sandwiches (salmon spread, cheese and tomato for Granny — peanut butter, honey and strawberry jam for Maisie), homemade cake, milk, a bottle of lemonade, and a flask of tea; Maisie's bathing costume, spade and pail, a bath towel and her yellow slicker and sou'wester (just in case); Granny's knitting and library book, a box of paper hankies and a packet of Pan Drops.

Mrs McKitty came to see if they were ready. Although it was another lovely, warm, sunny day, she was wearing her best fur coat and a new hat. She peered into the bag.

"I don't think you'll be needing Maisie's swimsuit," she sniffed. "I've been on Mystery Tours before, and they *always* go to Auchtermuchty, and there's no beach there."

Maisie's heart sank, but Granny zipped up the bag, winked at Maisie, and smiled.

"Well now, Marjorie McKitty," she said, "We'll just have to wait and see."

The bus was magnificent. It was large and luxurious, brightly painted and covered in gleaming chrome, with soft plush reclining seats and panels in the roof which opened, to let the sun shine in. Mr McMoggie, the driver, was also large — a tubby cat with great bushy whiskers and a deep fruity chortle. He welcomed all the passengers and showed them to their seats. Soon, the bus was filled with lots of excited cats and kittens, clutching spades and pails, fishing rods and nets, balloons, picnic hampers and carrier bags. Once everyone was aboard, Mr McMoggie shouted, "We're off," and to the cheers of the kittens, started the bus on its road to adventure.

They quickly left the city behind and wound along country roads until they reached the great Forth Bridge. As they crossed over the river, which sparkled with sunshine far below them, the kittens whooped and whistled with glee, and Mrs McKitty nodded to Granny.

"Mark my words, Isabella," she said, confidently. "As sure as little green

apples, we'll turn left at the other side and end up at Auchtermuchty. You'll see."

The bus turned right, and Granny smiled to herself. It cruised past herds of black and white cows, verges of white daisies and scarlet poppies and, sometimes, when the road swung near the sea, they caught glimpses of seals sunning themselves on salt-streaked rocks. The bus came to a stop in a little town and Mr McMoggie stood up at the front.

"Special stop at Burntisland," he called, over the murmers of his passengers. "Ice creams on the house, for kittens only!"

There was a great cheer, and with hurrah's and yippee's, the smaller passengers piled out of the bus and into an Ice Cream Parlour, to emerge minutes later carrying huge dripping cones and wafers, white and pink, with raspberry and chocolate sauce and liberally sprinkled with hundreds and thousands. They took their seats, and off the bus went again on its mysterious journey.

It followed the coast road until it reached a bigger town, and stopped once more.

"Twenty minute stop at Kirkcaldy," announced Mr McMoggie. "Famous for linoleum and the Green Cockatoo Cafe — excellent tea and buns laid on!"

This time, it was the older passengers' turn to be grateful. They climbed out of the bus and made their way along the busy High Street, looking at the shops. In the Cafe, Granny and Mrs McKitty had fresh scones with their tea and Mrs McKitty admitted that *this* Tour was a real mystery. Maisie was impatient at the delay, and she urged Granny to drink up, but before long everyone was back on board and the bus sped on.

"There's the statue of Robinson Crusoe," shouted Mr McMoggie, as he drove through the little fishing village of Lower Largo. Granny told Maisie the story about how Robinson Crusoe had been shipwrecked on a lonely desert island, and how he met Cat Friday. Maisie though of her Daddy and how close he had come to being shipwrecked.

Now there was a salty tang in the air, a smell of fish and sea, as the bus swung down a narrow winding road and came to a halt.

"This is Crail," said Mr McMoggie. "We stop here for an hour, and you can buy fresh fish at the quayside, and take a trip round the bay."

The cats and kittens stretched their legs. Granny bought some crab at a stall, and Mrs McKitty got some pink lobster for her Sunday tea. Then they took Maisie down to the harbour steps, where several others from the bus were already clambering into a little boat. Granny made Maisie put on her slicker and sou' wester, while she and Mrs McKitty pinned on their hats in case they blew into the sea. The boat — *The Sally Ann* — sailed out of the harbour and into open water.

It was choppy out here. The wind was strong and the waves grew higher as they went further from the shore. A funny look crept over the faces of Granny, Mrs McKitty and some of the other, older, passengers. They sat tight in their seats, kept their eyes shut, and gripped the side rails tight. The kittens, however, loved every minute of the short voyage. They waved to others on land, squawked back at the seagulls soaring overhead, shouted with joy when one spotted a porpoise — dipping in and out of the water to starboard — and thoroughly enjoyed the experience.

Maisie wondered if there would be a storm, if they'd be shipwrecked on the island nearby, if there would be a Cat Friday on it! But the little boat rounded the island safely and took them all back to harbour. Granny said that she had never been so happy to see dry land, and Mrs McKitty, for once, said nothing.

Back in the bus, Mr McMoggie checked that no-one had been left behind, and drove them out of Crail, towards their mysterious destination. It was almost lunchtime, when he parked the bus beside a beach, called for silence and told them that they were at St Andrews — this was it! Mrs McKitty couldn't believe it.

All the mums and dads, grannies and grandpas, kittens large and small, made their way towards the sand. While Granny unpacked the picnic, Maisie put on her costume and, after she had quickly munched her sandwiches and drunk her milk, she built a huge sandcastle with her spade and pail. Some smaller kittens helped her and dug a moat right round it, which Maisie filled with sea-water. Then Granny persuaded Mrs McKitty to take off her fur coat and go for a paddle (but she kept her hat pinned firmly on).

Maisie really didn't like water *at all* and very hesitantly tiptoed to the edge. In fact, it was only the sight of Granny and Mrs McKitty, quite out of character, paddling in the shallows that decided Maisie to venture in. Cautiously, she dipped one paw in. Gingerly, she stepped forward with the other.

"Yowwwl!" Maisie screeched. She hopped from one paw to the other, lost her balance and tumbled, with a splash, right into a breaker. Granny hurried over to see what was up.

"Look, Granny, look!" squealed Maisie, "a crab, a crab!"
And sure enough, a big pink crab had caught her paw. Granny took it off and kissed the paw better, and Maisie went back to the beach to play, vowing that she would never, *ever,* go in the sea again.

Later, they went for a game of Pitch and Putt.

"St Andrews is famous as the home of golf," Mrs McKitty told Maisie.
She appeared to know a lot about it. She told Maisie and Granny — who admitted to knowing nothing of the game — all about the Open Championship and about the famous golfers she had met when her dear late husband, Cecil, had been Captain of his Club. It seemed that golf was an approved pastime in the McKitty family and Mrs McKitty promised that she would see them "all right."
She showed Maisie how to hold her club and explained how to swing it and told her that she was to try to knock the ball into a hole, in the least number of strokes. Maisie swung, hit . . . . and got a hole in one. Mrs McKitty didn't seem too pleased.

"Beginner's luck," she sniffed.
Granny swung her club, and missed. Twice. Then she managed to hit the ball a few yards. Granny really wasn't too bothered.
Then Mrs McKitty took up her position. She lined up her ball, eyed the flag, took a practice swing, and then swung for real. The ball soared high in the air. They followed its course with amazement. It hit the greenkeeper on the head!
Maisie could not contain herself and collapsed in a giggling heap, as the furious greenkeeper marched up and gave Mrs McKitty a good telling-off.

"You should be ashamed of yourself,' he roared. "We don't want hooligans like *you* in St Andrews! You are a danger to the public. Get off my course at once! Go back where you belong!" And with that, he confiscated Mrs McKitty's clubs and strode away.

In silence, Mrs McKitty walked into town with Granny and Maisie. They had a dander round the shops, looking at this and that and buying a few small souvenirs to take home. Maisie got some picture postcards for her friends and her Daddy, and then they joined a party from the bus who were just setting out with Mr McMoggie for a guided tour of the old Castle. By the time they reached it, Granny was feeling a bit puffed-out, so she and Mrs McKitty found a bench and sat outside in the sun, to rest their weary paws, while Maisie and the others went inside.

It was dark and cool, and Mr McMoggie led the party through old rooms, telling them something of their history. Maisie noticed some words scratched on a wall and stopped to examine them — it was a date and a name, Mary something or other, but so worn that it was difficult to decipher.

When Maisie turned around, she found that the party had gone. She was quite alone. She began to search for the others, but found herself going deeper and deeper into the ruins. At length she found herself in a dark, dark chamber, with damp, dripping walls and no way to go further.

"I'll just have to re-trace my steps," she thought. But she found that a great, rusty iron door had swung shut behind her. She was trapped!

Maisie banged and kicked at the door, squeaking and squealing as she clawed at it. The handle was high above her head and, jump as she might, she just couldn't reach it.

"Maybe they'll all go back to Edinburgh without me," she thought. "Maybe I'll be stuck here for ever!" She began to sob and whimper, when suddenly, she felt a draft and turned to see the figure of a lady cat, standing in the darkest corner of the chamber.

"Oh, please help me," begged Maisie. "I can't reach the handle."

The figure glided silently past Maisie, reached out its paw, turned the handle and opened the door.

"Oh, thankyou," gasped Maisie. "I was so frightened, I didn't realize that you were there."

And as she spoke, she saw the lady cat, in her long velvet dress, walk through one of the cold, wet walls, moaning softly as she disappeared.

It was a GHOST!

Maisie moaned too. Her fur rose and her tail fluffed out like a brush. Her eyes nearly popped out of her head. She took to her heels and ran headlong through tunnels and chambers until, panting, gasping and squealing, she found herself out in the warm afternoon sun. There were the other cats and kittens! There was Mr McMoggie, beaming and chortling! And there were Granny and Mrs McKitty!

Maisie ran to them and spilled out her story.

"Och, Maisie," said Granny, rocking her on her knee, "It's all right, pet. It's just your imagination."

"Too much sunshine," agreed Mrs McKitty. "Too much ice cream."

On the road back home, Mr McMoggie stopped the bus at Pittenweem and everyone got fish suppers in "The Best Fish Restaurant in Scotland." Or so he called it. Maisie munched her supper and began to feel much more cheerful. And then they were back in Morningside, tired and happy, with Mrs McKitty's embarrassment and Maisie's fright almost forgotten.

Before going to bed, Maisie wrote her postcards, telling her friends about *her* holiday and telling her Daddy that she *had* seen a ghost. Granny made the cocoa and they sat together, gazing out of the window at the rosy sky.

"Did you enjoy the Mystery Tour, Maisie," asked Granny.

"Oh, yes," said Maisie, enthusiastically. "I don't feel at all down in the dumps now."

"That's good," agreed Granny. She looked at the sunset. "I think it'll be another fine day tomorrow."

"I hope so," said Maisie. "There's so much I want to do."